The Muppet Babies live in a nursery
in a house on a street that is a lot like yours.
But they can travel anywhere anytime using a special power—
the power of the imagination.
Can you imagine what it would be like to go with them?
Join the Muppet Babies on this adventure and find out.

Weekly Reader Presents

Baby Fozzie
Is Afraid of the Dark

By Marilyn Kaye • Illustrated by Tom Brannon

Muppet Press • New York

Weekly Reader Books offers several exciting
card and activity programs. For information,
write to WEEKLY READER BOOKS, P.O. Box 16636,
Columbus, Ohio 43216.

This book is a presentation of
Weekly Reader Books.

Weekly Reader Books offers book clubs for children
from preschool through high school.

For further information write to:
Weekly Reader Books
4343 Equity Drive
Columbus, Ohio 43228

Weekly Reader is a trademark of Field Publications.

Printed in the United States of America

It was the middle of the night in the nursery. The room was dark, and all the Muppet Babies were in their cribs, fast asleep. All, that is, except one.

Baby Fozzie was sitting straight up, and his eyes were wide open. His little shoulders were shaking. He felt cold, then hot, then cold again.

Poor Baby Fozzie was afraid of the dark.
What made it worse was there was no one to talk
to. Fozzie felt like he was the only one in the whole
wide world who was awake.

He wished Baby Kermit would wake up.
Kermit was so brave! He wasn't afraid of the dark.

"Kermit," Fozzie whispered. "Please wake up." But
Kermit went right on sleeping.

"Kermit," Fozzie begged a little louder. But Kermit
just lay there.

"KERMIT!" Fozzie yelled.

Kermit's eyes popped open. "Huh? What?"
"Gee, Kermit," Fozzie said, trying to sound sur-
prised. "Did I wake you up?"

"Yes, you did," Kermit grumbled. "And I was having a great dream. Why aren't you sleeping?"

Fozzie was ashamed to tell Kermit that he was afraid of the dark. So he answered, "Uh, I was too cold."

"Then get under your blanket," Kermit said.

"Uh, maybe I had too much to eat," Fozzie said.

"You always have too much to eat."

"Uh, maybe I'm just a little bit afraid of the dark."

"That's silly," mumbled Kermit sleepily. "Now go to sleep so I can go back to my dream."

"What are you dreaming about, Kermit?" asked Fozzie. He didn't want Kermit to fall asleep again.

Kermit yawned and closed his eyes. "I'm in a flying boat. It's about to go sailing through the night."

"Through the night! In the dark!" Fozzie exclaimed. "Aren't you scared?"

"There's nothing to be scared of," Kermit replied. "It's fun."

"What does the boat look like?" asked Fozzie, trying to keep Kermit up longer.

"Sort of like this crib, only it's all silver and gold."

"Where is the boat going, Kermit?"
"It's sailing out the window."
"Don't leave me here. Can't I come with you, Kermit?"
"Sure, Fozzie. We're on our way!"

Outside the nursery, the boat sailed slowly down the
street and across town.

"Hey, Kermit, what's that man doing down there in
the dark?"

"He's a night watchman," Kermit said. "He guards
that factory after dark."

The boat rose higher and circled over the city.
Fozzie shivered. "Kermit, it's so dark up here!"

"It's not dark down there." Kermit pointed.
"Look!"

Fozzie looked down. There were lights shining all
over the city.

"Why do all those buildings have their lights on?" Fozzie asked. "I thought everyone was asleep at night."

"Oh, no," Kermit said. "That's a police station, and there's a fire station, and over there is a hospital. There are people in those buildings who work all night."

The boat floated on, past the city and over a forest.
Fozzie shivered again. "Kermit, it's so lonely and
empty down there."

"No, it isn't," Kermit said. "Look!"

A yellow-eyed owl perched on a tree, while a small brown bat flew through the branches.

"Why aren't they sleeping?" Fozzie asked.

"Lots of animals stay up at night," Kermit explained. "That's when they hunt for food."

"I'm glad I'm not an owl or a bat," Fozzie said. "I still don't like the night. It's not as special as daytime." Kermit just smiled and said, "Look up."

Fozzie looked up. Above them, thousands of stars were twinkling in the clear, dark sky. "Gee, Kermit," sighed Fozzie, "that's really beautiful!"

"And if there wasn't any darkness," said Kermit, "we wouldn't be able to see those stars."

But Fozzie was still worried. Where did the sun go when the dark came? And what if the sun never came back?

Their boat rose higher and higher. It began moving faster and faster. Soon the earth looked like a large ball beneath them.

"Hey, Kermit," Fozzie yelled. "Look! It's getting lighter over there!"

"We're on the other side of the world now," Kermit said. "When it's dark over the nursery, it's light over here. When we have nighttime, the people here have daytime."

Fozzie peered down from the boat. He saw streets, parks, buildings, beaches, and lots of people in the bright sunlight.

Kermit turned the boat around, and they sailed back into the dark. Before long, they were at the forest where the owls and the bats were wide awake. They sailed over the police station, the fire station, and the hospital, where people worked all night. Finally, they floated back through the nursery window.

"That was a good trip, Kermit," Fozzie said. "I guess the dark isn't so scary after all. I thought I was alone, but there are people working, and animals hunting for food, and on the other side of the world, the children are outside playing."

Kermit didn't answer. He was fast asleep, dreaming.

And, finally, so was Baby Fozzie.